Please Take

ALFRED A. KNOPF
NEW YORK

Me for a Walk

Susan Gal

Please take me for a walk.

I need to chase away the neighbors' cat,

send the birds back to their nests,

and keep the squirrels high up in the trees.

Please take me for a walk.

I like to greet the people on my street.

Some neighbors like to pet me,

and some neighbors do not.

Please take me for a walk.

I want to say hello to

the florist,

the greengrocer,

the baker,

the bookseller,

and my special friend, the butcher.

Please take me for a walk.

I like to watch the kids in the schoolyard,

the guys shooting hoops,

and the people playing chess.

Please take me for a walk.

I could catch a ball for you,

retrieve a Frisbee,

and race you to the water fountain.

Please take me for a walk.

I want to feel
the wind lift my ears

and the sun warm my belly.

Please take me for a walk
so I can meet other dogs,

and other dogs
can meet me.

Please take me for a walk
so everyone can see . . .

. . . my best friend and me.

For my best friend, Wanda Woo—S.G.

THIS IS A BORZOI BOOK PUBLISHED BY ALFRED A. KNOPF

Copyright © 2010 by Susan Gal

All rights reserved. Published in the United States by Alfred A. Knopf, an imprint of Random House Children's Books, a division of Random House, Inc., New York.

Knopf, Borzoi Books, and the colophon are registered trademarks of Random House, Inc.

Visit us on the Web! www.randomhouse.com/kids

Educators and librarians, for a variety of teaching tools, visit us at www.randomhouse.com/teachers

Library of Congress Cataloging-in-Publication Data
Gal, Susan.
Please take me for a walk / by Susan Gal. — 1st ed.
p. cm.
Summary: A dog gives many good reasons it likes to go for a walk—to chase away the neighbor's cat,
to greet people on the street, to watch guys shooting hoops, and to feel the wind lifting its ears.
ISBN 978-0-375-85863-5 (trade) — ISBN 978-0-375-95863-2 (lib. bdg.)
[1. Dogs—Fiction. 2. Dog walking—Fiction.] I. Title.
PZ7.G12964Pl 2010
[E]—dc22
2009022083

The illustrations in this book were created using
charcoal on paper and digital collage.

MANUFACTURED IN MALAYSIA
May 2010
10 9 8 7 6 5 4 3 2 1
First Edition